To Xander, Otto and Baby Dexter –
Always be kind, help others whenever you can,
and never miss a chance to play in the snow. – P.C.

HODDER CHILDREN'S BOOKS

First published in Great Britain in 2021
by Hodder and Stoughton

Text and illustrations © Pippa Curnick 2021

A CIP catalogue record of this book
is available from the British Library.

HB ISBN: 978 1 444494 879 0
PB ISBN: 978 1 444494 880 6

10 9 8 7 6 5 4 3 2 1

Printed and bound in China.

MIX
Paper from
responsible sources
FSC® C104740

Hodder Children's Books
An imprint of
Hachette Children's Group
Part of Hodder and Stoughton
Carmelite House
50 Victoria Embankment
London, EC4Y 0DZ

An Hachette UK Company
www.hachette.co.uk
www.hachettechildrens.co.uk

"They're MAGNIFICENT!"
said Shama and Bahama.

"Truly FABULOUS!"
agreed Penguin and Rabbit.

"They're PAW-FECT!"
agreed Bear.

"Now we're ready to . . .

"Don't worry," said Shama.
"We're experts in working together.
Making sweaters will be easy-peasy."

"I can sew!"
said Bahama.

"I'll do
sparkles,"
said Penguin.

"I can make
pom-poms!"
said Rabbit.

"We could use these
pine cones?"
said Bear.

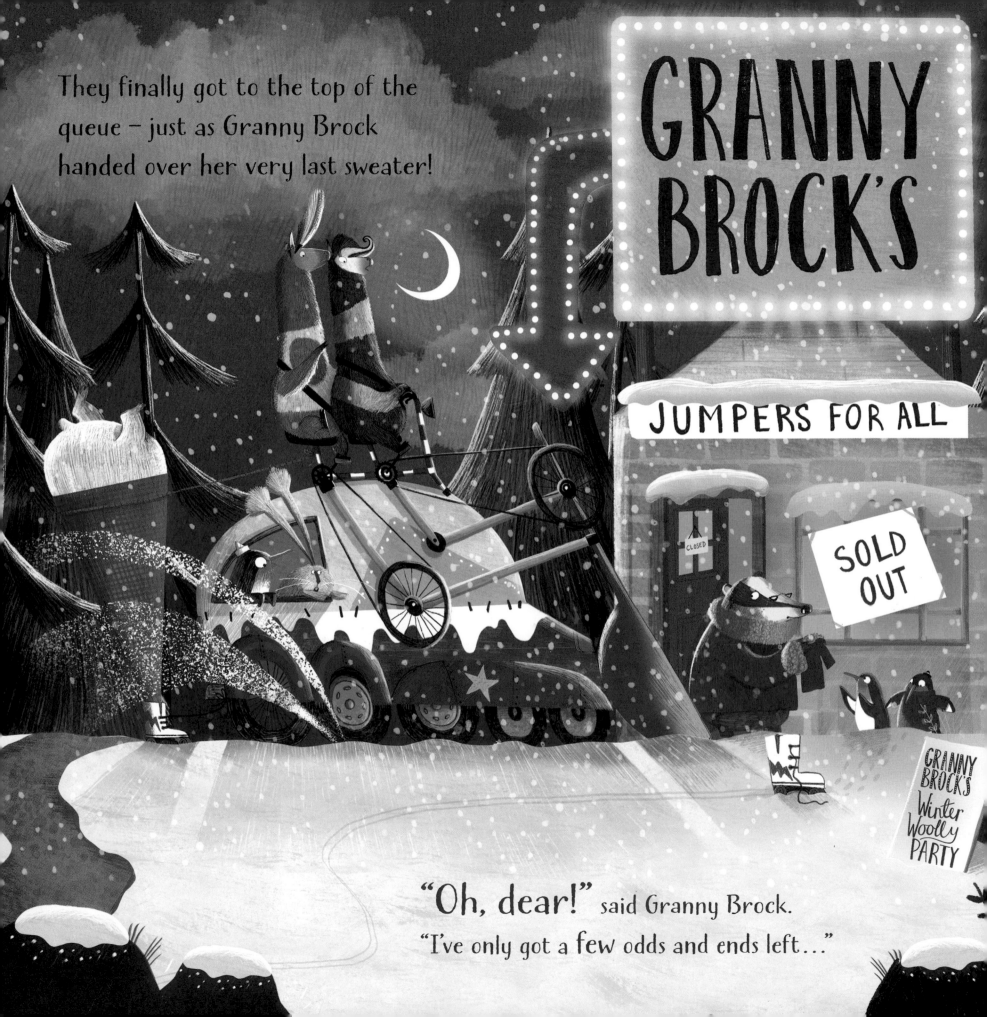

They finally got to the top of the queue – just as Granny Brock handed over her very last sweater!

GRANNY BROCK'S

JUMPERS FOR ALL

SOLD OUT

CLOSED

GRANNY BROCK'S Winter Woolly PARTY

"Oh, dear!" said Granny Brock.
"I've only got a few odds and ends left..."

BUT – OH NO! It looked like they
still hadn't managed to beat the queue.

One little push and the snowmobile swept down the hill towards Granny Brock's shop. Faster and **faster** it **zoomed** along in a **swoosh** of swirling snowflakes.

together they built a SNAZZTASTIC, SUPER-SPEEDY SNOWSCOOP!

And so, bit by bit...

with a few mistakes...

HELP!

HELP!

and a few debates...

"We can build something from all these broken bits to get us to Granny Brock's shop."

"We'll **NEVER** get to Granny Brock's before she sells all her jumpers," wailed Bear.

"It's all **YOUR** fault!"

"I beg your pardon?" cried Penguin.

"We'll all turn into icicles!" shrieked Rabbit.

UH-OH. Now they were all well and truly stuck.

It was an ICE-CREAM AVALANCHE!

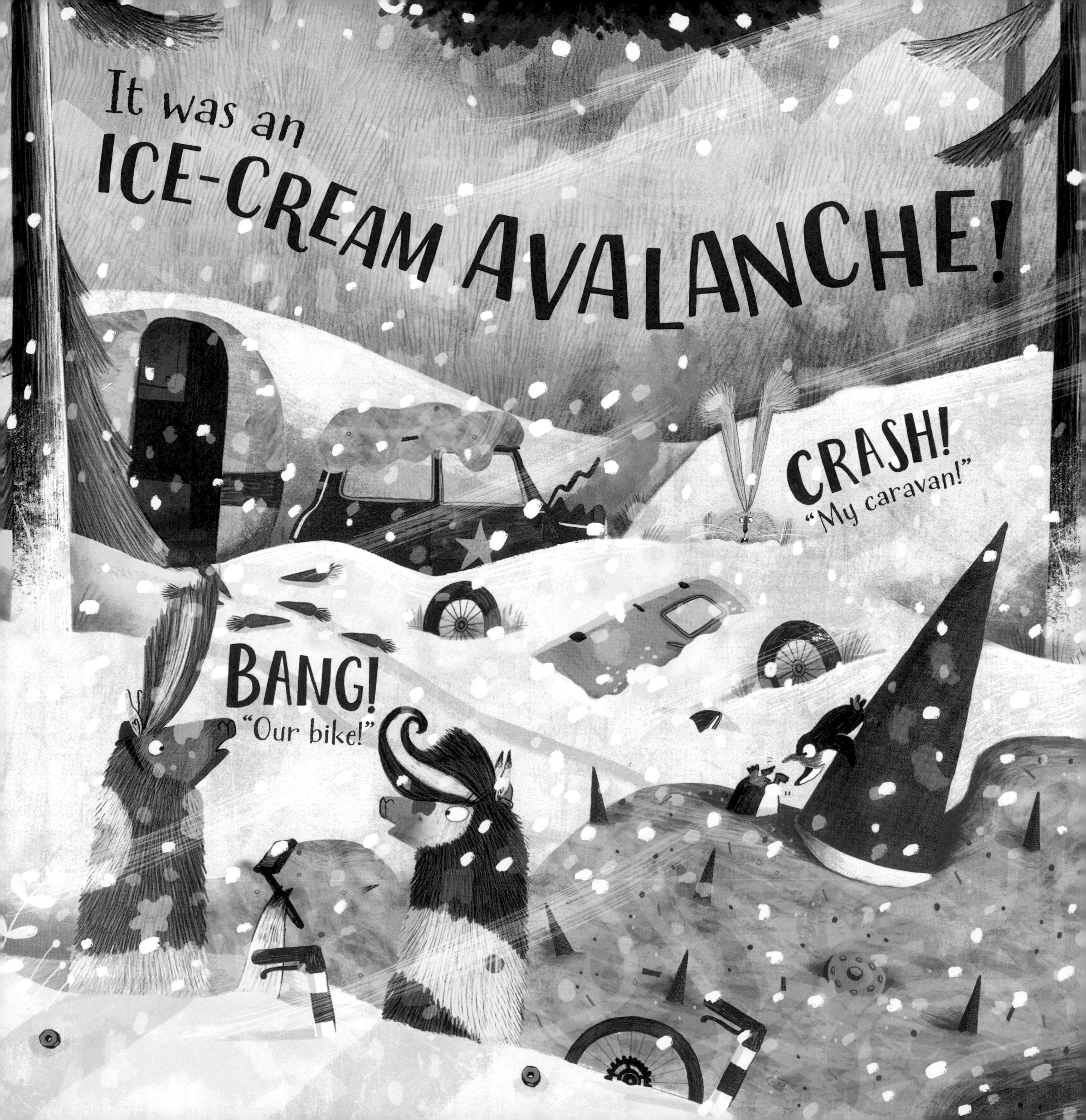

Penguin couldn't see a thing! She reached for the brake but accidentally pulled the ICE-CREAM-RELEASE LEVER!

OH NO!

But before they knew it, the wind began to blow and the first raindrops fell.

The rain turned to hail and then to snow.

And **BEAR** was bumping ahead on his skates.
They all wanted to be the first to get one
of Granny Brock's new-season sweaters!

But everyone else had the same idea.

RABBIT was rushing along with his caravan.

PENGUIN was pushing past in her ice-cream van.

"TO GRANNY BROCK'S JUMPER SHOP!" cried Shama and Bahama, hopping on their bike. And off they sped.

The naughty moths had chomped right through their winter woollies – they were full of holes!

There was only one thing for it . . .

Shama and Bahama
jumped for **joy**.

They couldn't wait to put
on their snuggly sweaters.

But there was a **nasty surprise** waiting for them...

Our first jumpers

GRANNY BROCK'S

JUMPERS FOR ALL

OPEN

Granny Brock's Shop

But this year, it was beginning to look like the snow would never come — and that meant **NO PARTY!**

. . . THE WINTER WOOLLY PARTY!"

GRANNY BROCK'S
Winter Woolly
PARTY
- ADMIT ONE -

Winter Woolly
Party

All the animals loved the Winter Woolly Party – it was the best night
of the year! And everyone knew that Granny Brock's shop was the
very best place to purchase a snuggly sweater.

"Twinkly lights and hot chocolate,"
dreamed Bahama. "And best of all . . .

"I think I'm melting!" moaned Shama Llama.

"We llamas are not built for this kind of heat," said Bahama Llama.

"We're much too woolly! When is it going to be nice and chilly again?"

They decided it might be best to go indoors to cool off.

"I can't wait for it to start snowing," said Bahama.
"I can't wait for skating and snowballs," said Shama.

It was the end of a very long summer,
and the sun was showing no sign of cooling down.
All the animals were feeling sweaty and sticky
and **MUCH TOO HOT!**

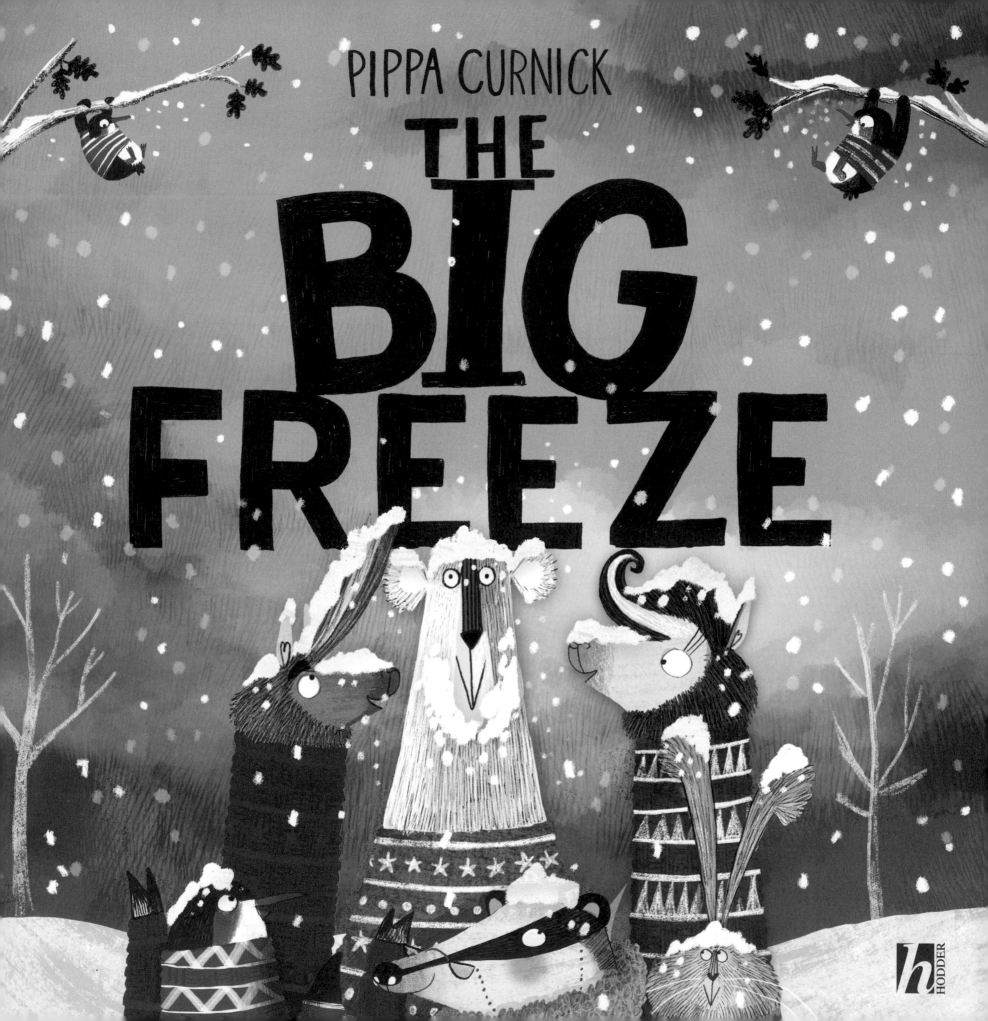